This book belongs to
my friend:

_____

A NOTE TO PARENTS

Blue and her friends discover that the world is full of vibrant colors in *The Color Finders*. Learning to identify colors is an enjoyable and fairly easy skill to master for most children.

As you read the book, play an eye-spy game along with Blue. Search each page for the colorful fruit that is hinted at by Mr. Salt and Mrs. Pepper's riddles. On each page, direct your child to find other items of the same color as the fruit that is featured. Also encourage your child to look for objects at home that match the colors Blue and Magenta search for in the story.

After you finish the book, try exploring colors in other ways. For starters, have your child help you make a colorful fruit salad—just like Mr. Salt and Mrs. Pepper's surprise! Cut out pictures from magazines that highlight each color, and make a colorful collage on construction paper or poster board. Or, encourage your child to mix colors to create "new" colors, using crayons, colored pencils, pastels, finger paints, or other paints. Then illustrate scenes from the book or paint your own colorful creations.

Learning Fundamental:　　　　　color + shape

For more parent and kid-friendly activities, go to www.nickjr.com.

The Color Finders

Colorful Surprise!

© 2003 Viacom International Inc. All Rights Reserved. Nickelodeon, Nick Jr., Blue's Clues and all related titles, logos and characters are trademarks of Viacom International Inc.

No part of this publication may be reproduced in whole or in part, or stored in a retrieval system, or transmitted in any form or by any means, electronic, mechanical, photocopying, recording, or otherwise, without written permission of the publisher.

Published by Scholastic Inc., 90 Old Sherman Turnpike, Danbury, CT 06816

SCHOLASTIC and associated logos are trademarks and/or registered trademarks of Scholastic Inc.

ISBN 0-7172-6627-3

Printed in the U.S.A.

First Scholastic Printing, February 2003

The Color Finders

by
Annie Evans

illustrated by
Tom Mangano

SCHOLASTIC INC.

New York Toronto London Auckland Sydney
Mexico City New Delhi Hong Kong Buenos Aires

"Guess what?" Mr. Salt asked Blue and Magenta. "We are all going to the Color Fair this afternoon!" "Hooray!" Blue and Magenta shouted.

"We want to make a surprise to take with us," Mrs. Pepper said. "Will you help us find everything we need?"

"Sure!" Blue said. "We'd like to help."

"We need lots of different colors for the surprise," explained Mrs. Pepper.

"We can be the Color Finders!" Magenta said excitedly.

Colorful Surprise!

"Wonderful," Mr. Salt said. "The first item on our list is red, and it should also be round and crunchy."
"Let's check the backyard," Blue suggested.

"We are looking for something red, round,
and crunchy," Magenta told Shovel and Pail.
"I'm red and round," said Pail.
"Yes," Blue agreed, "but you aren't crunchy."

"Maybe what you want is around here somewhere," suggested Shovel.
Everyone peered around the yard.
"I see it!" cried Magenta.

"We found some apples! They're red, round, and crunchy," Magenta told Mr. Salt and Mrs. Pepper. "*Magnifique!*" said Mrs. Pepper, clapping her hands together.

Colorful Surprise!

"Now we need something that is blue, round, and small," said Mr. Salt.

"Let's try the garden," Blue suggested.

On their way to the garden, Blue and Magenta saw Periwinkle playing in his yard.

"We're Color Finders," Magenta told Periwinkle.

"We're looking for something blue, round, and small," Blue explained.

"Your ball is blue and round," Periwinkle pointed out.
"But it's big, not small," Magenta giggled.
Suddenly Blue shouted, "I found it! Did you?"

"Here are some blueberries. They're blue, round, and small!" Blue told Mr. Salt and Mrs. Pepper.

"*Merci!*" sang Mrs. Pepper. "Something yellow is next. It's also long and needs to be peeled."

"Hmm. We'll have to think about this," Blue said.

Colorful Surprise!

The Color Finders sat in the Thinking Chair and thought about yellow things.

"There are lots of yellow things in here," Sidetable Drawer piped up.

"Yes," Blue agreed, "but it should also be long, and it needs to be peeled."

Magenta hopped off the chair with a gleeful shout, "I know what it is!"

"Here are some bananas," Magenta said to Mr. Salt and Mrs. Pepper. "They're yellow and long, and they need to be peeled."

Colorful Surprise!

"Wonderful," said Mrs. Pepper.

"We could also use something that is purple, round, and comes in bunches," Mr. Salt said.

"Let's look in the front yard," Blue suggested.

Periwinkle was collecting bugs on the front path. "Hi. Are you still Color Finders?" he asked.

"Yes," Magenta said. "Have you seen something purple and round that comes in bunches?"

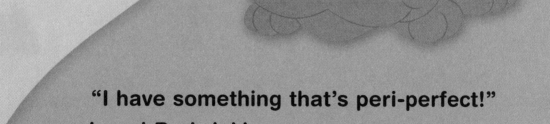

"I have something that's peri-perfect!" grinned Periwinkle.

"Oh, you're right, Periwinkle," Blue said.

"Here are some grapes. They're purple and round, and they come in bunches," Blue told Mr. Salt and Mrs. Pepper.

"These are perfect for the surprise," cheered Mr. Salt. "But we still need a few more colors."

Colorful Surprise!

"Can you find something that is green, sweet, and bigger on the bottom than it is on the top?" asked Mrs. Pepper.

"This hat is green and bigger on the bottom than it is on the top," Magenta told Blue.

"But it's not sweet," laughed Blue.

Suddenly Mailbox appeared in the window.
"The mail's here!" he called out.

"Thanks, Mailbox," Magenta said. "Oh! I think
I found the answer, Blue."

Mr. Salt
&
Mrs. Pepper

"Here are some pears," Magenta announced. "They are green, sweet, and bigger on the bottom than they are on the top."

"*Magnifique!*" said Mrs. Pepper. "There is just one more color on the list."

"We need something that is orange," said Mr. Salt.
"And round and juicy!" added Mrs. Pepper.
The Color Finders looked around.
"I already see it!" Blue shouted. "Do you?"

ORANGE

Colorful Surprise!

Blue raced across the kitchen with Magenta right behind her. Grandma Cayenne was giving Paprika and Cinnamon their lunch. Paprika was eating something orange, round, and juicy.

"Hi," Paprika said to Blue and Magenta. "Do you want an orange?"

The Color Finders nodded and smiled.

"*Merci,*" Mrs. Pepper said. "You found apples, blueberries, bananas, grapes, pears, and oranges."

"Now we are ready to make our surprise for the Color Fair," Mr. Salt said excitedly.

"What could it be?" Magenta whispered to Blue.

"It's time for the surprise!" Mr. Salt announced at the fair.

"*Voilà!*" said Mr. Pepper, uncovering a large bowl of fruit salad.

"Wow!" Blue exclaimed. "That's made with all the colorful things we found!"

Mrs. Pepper nodded and smiled. "We could not have made this colorful surprise without the help of the Color Finders."